Wilbie & Harry

For Claire, Rob, Andrew and Philip

MYRIAD BOOKS LIMITED
35 Bishopsthorpe Road, London SE26 4PA

First published in 2005 by
PICCADILLY PRESS LIMITED
5 Castle Road, London NW1 8PR
www.piccadillypress.co.uk

Text and illustrations copyright © Sally Chambers 2005

ISBN 1 905606 92 3
EAN 9 781905 606 924

Text designed by Sally Chambers and Louise Millar

Printed in China

Wilbie & Harry

Sally Chambers

MYRIAD BOOKS LIMITED

From the first time they met,
Wilbie and Harry had been the best of friends.

They had known each other since they were babies, and they did everything together.

They learned to walk together.

They learned
to talk together.

They went to school together.

They sat in
class together.

They walked home from
school together.

And they played
together all
the time.

Most of the time they played football.
At the bottom of Harry's garden was an old shed.
But this was not just any old shed.
This was Wilbie and Harry's den.

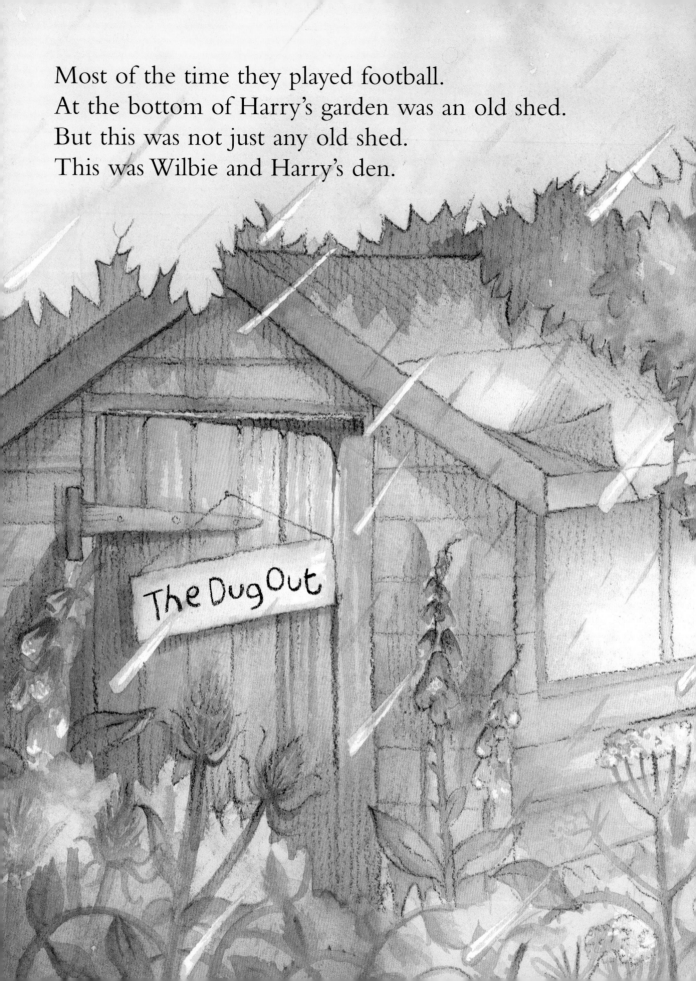

The Dug Out

If the weather was bad it was
their favourite place to play.

Wilbie and Harry loved their den.
Each week they saved some of their pocket money
and put it in a jar.
When the jar was full they would go to the shops
to buy special things for their special place.

When it rained, they would sit inside
the den, reading magazines and cutting
out pictures of their favourite teams.

One day, when the jar was
very full indeed, Wilbie took it
down from the shelf and he
and Harry went out as usual . . .

But today wasn't a usual day.
It was the day of the Grand School Fair.

Grand School Fair

Wilbie and Harry were very excited.

First they bought some
candy floss.

Then they tried to hook a fish.

They had a guess at the
weight of the cake.

And they even had a try at
the hoopla.

Soon the jar was looking quite empty.

Harry shook the money on to the grass.
"What shall we do next?" he asked as
he counted the coins.
"Look over there!" shouted Wilbie.
"A raffle to win a signed football!"

There was just enough money to buy two tickets.
Wilbie and Harry sat together on the grass and waited.
Finally it was time for the winning number to be called.
Wilbie held on tightly to his ticket. He was very excited.
"And the winning number is . . ."

"...one hundred and twenty-seven!"
Wilbie couldn't believe it.
His ticket had won!
He rushed up to collect the prize.

"We've won, we've won!"
shouted Harry as Wilbie
came back with the ball.

"But *my* ticket was the winner!" said Wilbie.
"The money was from the jar. We always
share treats from the jar," said Harry.
But it was too late. Wilbie was already
rushing home with the prize.

Wilbie was very proud of his new ball.

He showed it to his
mum and dad.

He showed it to his
aunt and uncle.

He showed it to his
next-door neighbour.

And he even showed it
to the postman!

At night he put the ball right
next to his bed so that when
he woke up in the morning, it
would be the first thing he saw.

The next day, Wilbie asked Harry if he wanted to come and play. But Harry said he didn't feel like playing.

So Wilbie took Harry his favourite book to read. But Harry said he had read it already.

And at teatime, Wilbie took Harry a piece of cake. But Harry said he didn't like cake.

On Monday, Harry wouldn't sit next to Wilbie in class.

And that week, he wouldn't walk home with Wilbie.

And the next weekend, Wilbie had to play football all on his own. Wilbie was very upset.

That night, he was so upset that he
couldn't sleep.
He lay awake staring at the ball.

He really missed the den.
But most of all, he missed Harry.
And so he decided what he must do . . .

As soon as it was morning,
Wilbie rushed round to Harry's house.
Harry was playing football on his own in the garden.

"I'm very sorry, Harry," said Wilbie,
creeping through the gate.
"I don't want the ball, I just want to be friends.
Please – I want you to have it."

It was a little time before Harry looked up. Wilbie felt
nervous, because he really wanted his friend back.
"Couldn't we share the ball?" Harry said finally.
"We could keep it in the the den with
all the other treats from the jar."

Wilbie was delighted.

Harry had been hoping that Wilbie would come round.
He didn't really want to be cross with him.
"I really missed coming to play with you," said Wilbie.
"I really missed you too," said Harry.

And they dashed off to choose an extra special spot in the den for their ball.

Wilbie had learnt that friends were special.
And he decided he didn't want to lose his ever again.